Who Took My Hairy Toe?

RETOLD BY **Shutta Crum**

ILLUSTRATED BY **Katya Krenina**

Albert Whitman & Company

Morton Grove, Illinois

Library of Congress Cataloging-in-Publication Data

Crum, Shutta.

Who took my hairy toe ? / retold by Shutta Crum ; illustrated by Katya Krenina.

p. cm.

Summary: An old man known for taking what isn't his picks up the wrong thing

one Halloween night, and its owner wants it back.

ISBN 0-8075-5972-5 (hardcover)

[1. Folklore — United States.

2. Halloween — Folklore.] I. Krenina, Katya, ill. II. Title.

PZ8.1.C8845 Wh 2001 [E] — dc21

2001000890

Published in 2001 by Albert Whitman & Company,

6340 Oakton Street, Morton Grove, Illinois 60053-2723.

Published simultaneously in Canada by

General Publishing, Limited, Toronto.

The paintings are rendered in gouache.

The display type is ITC Jiggery Pokery.

The text type is Clair Regular.

The design is by Scott Piehl.

For Gerry. Always.

—S.C.

To Svetochka, my little artist friend.

—K.K.

On All Hallows' Eve, when the wind is whipping through the gap and the trees are scratching at the sky, the folks round here say you can hear Old Tar Pockets screaming.

Old Tar Pockets was not his real name. That has long been forgot.

Some say he was just an old man living up the holler away from other folk. But they also say he was a greedy old man. Even, that it wasn't safe to say "Howdy!" to him without taking a good hold to your hat.

He met his ruination one Halloween. You see, he was prospecting for a little something handy by his neighbor's barn while the neighbor was tarring his roof. By the barn sat an open bucket of warmed-up tar. "I'd like to get me some of that tar," he thought. "Might come in right handy sometime."

Well, the old man looked around but couldn't find anything to put it in. So when his neighbor wasn't looking, he dipped a stick full of that soft, warm tar outta the bucket and plopped it right into his coat pocket!

That's how he got his name: Old Tar Pockets.

Then he spied a few scraggly sweet potato plants, the last of the season, in his neighbor's garden. So Old Tar Pockets began to dig. And . . . he dug up a hairy toe!

It was big and covered in coarse brown fur, with a long yellow toenail curving over at the end.

Well, the old man wasn't sure what he would do with it. But he did hold with the old saying, "Finders, keepers!" So he took that toe and stuffed it into his pocket.

Old Tar Pockets carried home those stolen, golden sweets and cooked himself up a mess o' greens and taters for supper. Then he remembered he had that toe.

He reached into his pocket, but couldn't pull it out. You see, the tar had cooled down and hardened up a bit, and that toe was stuck fast.

In fact, the old man couldn't get his hand out! His hand was stuck to the tar on the toe, and the toe was stuck to the tar in his pocket!

Old Tar Pockets decided to get ready for bed. Tomorrow, when the sun was out, he'd warm up his jacket, soften up the tar, and pull everything out as slick as you please!

But just then, the wind began to rise and whistle round the windows. Outside, the trees began to jerk about and claw at the sky.

And Old Tar Pockets heard a question on the voice of the wind. It hissed about the corners of the house. It asked,

"Who took my hairy toe?"

The old man opened the door and stared out into the dark woods beyond the house. "Aah! Just my imagination," he thought and turned to shut the door. Then he heard it again, louder and closer.

"Who took my hairy toe?"

Quickly he closed and barred the door with his free hand. He latched the windows and pulled the curtains. It was dark in the little house.

Still, the wind came in through the chinks in the walls. He could hear the question again and again, louder and coming closer.

"Who took my hairy toe?"

"Who took my hairy toe?"

Old Tar Pockets raked out the fire and stopped up the chimney with rags. Nothing was getting inside tonight!

But he heard the voice again, this time from just outside the door!

"Who took my hairy toe?"

Standing wild-eyed in the center of the room, the old man heard scratching at the latch, and the clacking of claws being drawn down the wood of the door.

Old Tar Pockets jumped into bed and yanked a quilt over his head. But he could still hear the question, first at one window, then another.

"Who took my hairy toe?"
"Who took my hairy toe?"

Suddenly a mountain-bending shriek of wind blew against the old house with such force that the door cracked and lay in two pieces — gaping open!

Just as quickly, the wind died down. In the hush that followed, the old man could hear his heart beating. And, he could hear the thump, scri-i-itch, thump, scra-a-pe of heavy feet approaching his bed in the dark.

"Who...took...my...hairy...toe?"

Old Tar Pockets couldn't take it any longer! He sat up in bed and stared at the darkest darkness he had ever known. Two fiery red eyes stared back. Then he smelt the foul breath and felt the sharp claws as the beast reached toward him.

The old man flipped back those covers with his one free hand and cried, "Here! Here it is! I've got it in my pocket! Take it!"

The great beast moaned. It had found its hairy toe, but the toe was stuck in Old Tar Pockets' pocket!

With a shriek, the great red-eyed beast grabbed the old man, and tucking him under its arm, ran out of the house and into the October night.

Now, when ghosts and goblins haunt the hills, and the wind is rising in the treetops, they say you can hear the shrieks of the angry beast. If you listen carefully, you can hear the old man's screams, too, as beast and man wander the valleys and ridges of the mountains — together.

The kindly folk here say, "Pay that no nevermind! It's just Old Tar Pockets getting his due."

I say, "Just as long as what's in your pocket is yours . . . I wouldn't worry about it."

Author's Note

During my years as a librarian and storyteller, I have had the wonderful experience of sharing folk tales with audiences of all ages. *Who Took My Hairy Toe?* is my version of a folk tale that has passed from one person to another for hundreds of years. Most folk tales have a long lineage, and one can see the resemblance of "The Hairy Toe" to other tales, such as the "Teeny Tiny Bone," a British folk tale that may have come to America with early settlers.

Between 1935 and 1943, writers working for the Federal Writer's Project recorded many folk tales. Writers talked to people in several states. They wrote down the life histories, customs, slave narratives, folklore, songs, and poems that they heard. Later, some of this material was published.

Walter McCanless, from Anson County, North Carolina, recorded a version of "The Hairy Toe" that he heard from his wife. She heard it during her childhood, in about 1882, from Dupris Knight, an African-American. This could mean that the story had found a home within the rich Southern storytelling traditions of African-Americans.

In 1949, "The Hairy Toe" appeared in an anthology by B. A. Botkin entitled *A Treasury of Southern Folklore* (Crown Publishers). Folklorist and anthologist M. A. Jagendorf also collected several versions of the tale. "The Tale of the Hairy Toe" is in his *Folk Stories of the South* (Vanguard Press, 1972). There, he mentions a similar tale he heard in Ohio called "Tailipoo."

Part of the joy of folklore is that people hear, change, make a tale their own, and then pass it on. You can do that, too. Enjoy this tale. Make it your own. Pass it on. Let it live for hundreds of years more.

— S. C.